SESAME STREET

Bert and Ernie's Great Adventures

The Pirate Map

Adapted by Kathryn Knight from the script by Billy Aronson

LEVEL **1** READER

Published by Dalmatian Press, LLC. All rights reserved.
Printed in Guangzhou, Guangdong, China.

The DALMATIAN PRESS name is a trademark of Dalmatian Publishing Group,
Franklin, Tennessee 37068-2068. 1-866-418-2572.

"Oh, we are two pirates!
Yes, we ARRR!" Ernie sang.

"With a map for gold!
And it cannot be far!"
Bert sang.

"It's not far at all, old buddy,"
said Ernie. "Ahoy! There is land!
I'll get out and tie up
the rowboat."

Ernie began to tie the rope.
Bert looked at the map.
Just then . . .

Zip! Zoom!
A monkey zipped by on a vine.
He grabbed the map!
Zip! Zoom!
He zipped away to a tree.
Oh, no!

"Give us that map!" Ernie yelled.
"Then we will give you
anything you want."

Oo-eee-oo-oo-ah.
The monkey slid down.
It took Bert's hat.
"My pirate hat!" said Bert.

Oo-eee-oo-oo-ah.
"My shiny sword!" said Bert.

Oo-eee-oo-oo-ah . . .

"My shirt! My pants!"
Bert yelled.

"Awww," said Ernie.
"The monkey wants
to be a pirate, Bert."

Pirate Bert had no pants,
but he had a map.

He said, "To find the gold,
jump across three rocks
in the water."

"Okay, pirates,"
said Ernie.
"JUMP!"

One . . .
Two . . .
Oo-eee-oo-oo-ah.
Three!

"Stop, monkey!
I cannot see!"
Bert said.

"Okay, pirates!"
said Ernie.
"Here we go!
Three big steps
to the big,
BIG head."

"There it is!"
said Bert.

Pirate Bert looked at the map.
"Look for the happy face.
Then dig for the gold," he said.

Oo-eee-oo-oo-ah!

"You found it!"
Bert and Ernie yelled.
"You found the happy face."

Dig dig dig dig!
Dig dig dig!

Wow!
A box!
A BIG box!

"It is a pirate chest!"
said Ernie. "ARRR!
It will have gold!"

They lifted the lid.
Did the chest have gold?
They looked in.

"ARRRGH!" Ernie cried.

The chest had . . .

"Socks! Oh, no!" said Ernie.

"I love socks," said Bert.
"Socks are better than gold.
What is better than socks?"

"Rubber duckies!" said Ernie.

Drip drip drip drip!
Drip drip drip!

"Uh-oh, Bert," said Ernie.
"Rain is on the way.
We must go!
Go to the rowboat."

Pirate Ernie began to run.

"Wait!" said Pirate Bert.
"We must take the socks."

Ernie smiled.
"Okay, old buddy.
If you like the socks,
we will take the socks."

Huff puff! Huff puff!
Oo-eee-oo-oo-ah!

The pirates pulled (*huff puff!*)
and pushed (*huff puff!*)
the box of socks (*oo-eee!*)
all the way (*oo-oo-ah!*)
to the water.

"Oh, no!" said Bert.
"The rowboat is not here!"

Drip drip drip drip!

"And the rain IS here!"
said Ernie. "What can we do?"

"Hmmm . . ." said Bert.
"We can try . . ."

" . . . a box and socks!"

"Heh heh heh,"
Ernie giggled.
"Good plan, Bert!
ARRR!"